IRISH LEGENDS FOR CHILDREN

28/3/96 .

To James, Matt, Brian

" Happy Dreams "

Love from

Gretta Gretta , your

cousins .

Irish Legends for Children

LADY GREGORY

ILLUSTRATED
by
FRANCES BOLAND

MERCIER PRESS

MERCIER PRESS
PO Box 5, 5 French Church Street, Cork
16 Hume Street, Dublin 2

ISBN 0 85342 920 0

These stories were originally published in *Gods and Fighting Men* in 1904.

A CIP catalogue record for this book is available from the British Library.

14 13 12 11 10 9 8 7 6 5

Printed in Ireland by Colour Books Ltd.

Contents

1

The Fate of
the Children of Lir

Now at the time when the Tuatha de Danaan chose a king for themselves after the battle of Tailltin, and Lir heard the kingship was given to Bodb Dearg, it did not please him, and he left the gathering without leave and with no word to any one; for he thought it was he himself had a right to be made king. But if he went away himself, Bodb was given the kingship none the less, for not one of the five begrudged it to him but only Lir. And it is what they determined, to follow after Lir, and burn down his house, and to attack himself with spear and sword, on account of his not giving obedience to the king they had chosen. 'We will not do that,' said Bodb Dearg, 'for that man would defend any place he is in; and besides that,' he said, 'I am none the less king over the Tuatha de Danaan, although he does not submit to me.'

All went on like that for a good while, but at last a great misfortune came on Lir, for his wife died after a sickness of three nights. That came very hard on Lir, and there was heaviness on his mind after her. There was great talk of the death of that woman in her own time.

The news of it was told all through Ireland, and it came to the house of Bodb, and the best of the Men of Dea were with him at that time. And Bodb said: 'If Lir had a mind for it,' he said, 'my help and my friendship would be good for him now, since his wife is not living to him. For I have here with me the three young girls of the best shape, and the best appearance, and the best name in all Ireland, Aobh, Aoife, and Ailbhe, the three daughters of Oilell of Aran, my own three nurselings.' The Men of Dea said it was a good thought he had, and that what he said was true.

Messages and messangers were sent then from Bodb Dearg to the place Lir was, to say that if he had a mind to join with the Son of the Dagda and to acknowledge his lordship, he would give him a foster-child of his foster-children. Lir thought well of the offer, and he set out on the morrow with fifty chariots from Sidhe Fionn-achaidh; and he went by every short way till he

8

came to Bodb's dwelling-place at Loch Dearg, and there was a welcome before him there, and all the people were merry and pleasant before him, and he and his people got good attendance that night.

The three daughters of Oilell of Aran were sitting on the one seat with Bodb Dearg's wife, the queen of the Tuatha de Danaan, that was their foster-mother. And Bodb said: 'You may have your choice of the three young girls, Lir.'

'I cannot say,' said Lir, 'which one of them is my choice, but which ever of them is the eldest, she is the noblest, and it is best for me to take her.'

'If that is so,' said Bodb, 'it is Aobh is the eldest, and she will be given to you, if it is your wish.'

'It is my wish,' he said. And he took Aobh for his wife that night, and he stopped there for a fortnight, and then he brought her away to his own house, till he would make a great wedding-feast.

In the course of time Aobh brought forth two children, a daughter and a son, Fionnuala and Aodh their names were. After a while she was brought to bed again, and this time she gave birth to two sons, and they called them Fiachra

9

and Conn. She herself died at their birth, and that weighed very heavy on Lir, and only for the way his mind was set on his four children he would have gone near to die of grief.

The news came to Bodb Dearg's place, and all the people gave out three loud, high cries, keening their nurseling. And after they keened her it is what Bodb Dearg said: 'It is a fret to us our daughter to have died, for her own sake and for the sake of the good man we gave her to, for we are thankful for his friendship and his faithfulness. However,' he said, 'our friendship with one another will not be broken, for I will give him for a wife her sister Aoife.'

When Lir heard that, he came for the girl and married her, and brought her home to his house. There was honour and affection with Aoife for her sister's children; and indeed no person at all could see those four children without giving them the heart's love.

Bodb Dearg used often to be going to Lir's house for the sake of those children; and he used to bring them to his own place for a good length of time, and then he would let them go back to their own place again. The Men of Dea were at that time using the Feast of Age in every hill of the Sidhe in turn; and when they came to

Lir's hill those four children were their joy and delight, for the beauty of their appearance; and it is where they used to sleep, in beds in sight of their father Lir. He used to rise up at the break of every morning, and to lie down among his children.

But it is what came of all this, that a fire of jealousy was kindled in Aoife, and she got to have a dislike and a hatred of her sister's children.

Then she let on to have a sickness, that lasted through nearly the length of a year. At the end of that time she did a deed of jealousy and cruel treachery against the children of Lir.

One day she got her chariot yoked, and she took the four children in it, and they went forward towards the house of Bodb Dearg; but Fionnuala had no mind to go with her, for she knew by her she had some plan for their death or their destruction, and she had seen in a dream that there was treachery against them in Aoife's mind. But all the same she was not able to escape from what was before her.

When they were on their way Aoife said to her people: 'Let you kill now,' she said, 'the four children of Lir, for whose sake their father has given up my love, and I will give you your own choice of a reward out of all the good things of the world.'

'We will not do that indeed,' said they, 'and it is a bad deed you have thought of, and harm will come to you out of it.'

When they would not do as she bade them, she took out a sword herself to put an end to the children with; but she being a woman and with no good courage, and with no great strength in her mind, she was not able to do it.

They went on then west to Loch Dairbhreach, the Lake of the Oaks, and the horses were stopped there, and Aoife bade the children of Lir to go out and bathe in the lake, and they did as she bade them. As soon as Aoife saw them out in the lake she struck them with a Druid rod, and put on them the shape of four swans, white and beautiful. And it is what she said: 'Out with you, children of the king, your luck is taken away from you for ever; it is sorrowful the story will be to your friends; it is with flocks of birds your cries will be heard for ever.'

And Fionnuala said: 'Witch, we know now what your name is, you have struck us down with no hope of relief; but although you put us from wave to wave, there are times when we

will touch the land. We shall get help when we are seen; help, and all that is best for us: even though we have to sleep upon the lake, it is our minds will be going abroad early.'

Then the four children of Lir turned towards Aoife, and it is what Fionnuala said: 'It is a bad deed you have done, Aoife, and it is a bad fulfilling of friendship, you to destroy us without cause; and vengeance for it will come upon you, and you will fall in satisfaction for it, for your power for our destruction is not greater than the power of our friends to avenge it on you; and put some bounds now,' she said, 'to the time this enchantment is to stop on us.'

'I will do that,' said Aoife, 'and it is worse for you, you to have asked it of me. And the bounds I set to your time are this, till the Woman from the South and the Man from the North will come together. And since you ask to hear it of me,' she said, 'no friends and no power that you have will be able to bring you out of these shapes you are in through the length of your lives, until you have been three hundred years on Loch Dairbhreach, and three hundred years on Sruth na Maoile between Ireland and Alban, and three hundred years at Irrus Domnann and Inis Gluaire; and these are

14

to be your journeys from this out,' she said.

But then repentance came on Aoife, and she said: 'Since there is no other help for me to give you now, you may keep your own speech; and you will be singing sweet music of the Sidhe, that would put the men on the earth to sleep, and there will be no music in the world equal to it; and your own sense and your own nobility will stay with you, the way it will not weigh so heavy on you to be in the shape of birds. And go away out of my sight now, children of Lir,' she said, 'with your white faces, with your stammering Irish. It is a great curse on tender lads, they to be driven out on the rough wind. Nine hundred years to be on the water, it is a long time for any one to be in pain; it is I put this on you through treachery, it is best for you to do as I tell you now.

'Lir, that got victory with so many a good cast, his heart is a kernal of death in him now; the groaning of the great hero is a sickness to me, though it is I that have well earned his anger.'

Then the horses were caught for Aoife, and the chariot yoked for her, and she went on to the palace of Bodb Dearg, and there was a welcome before her from the chief people of the place. The son of the Dagda asked her why she did not bring the children of Lir with her. 'I will tell you that,' she said. 'It is because Lir has no liking for you, and he will not trust you with his children, for fear you might keep them from him altogether.'

'I wonder at that,' said Bodb Dearg, 'for those children are dearer to me than my own children,' and he thought in his own mind it was deceit the woman was doing on him, and it is what he did, he sent messengers to the north to Sidhe Fionnachaidh.

Lir asked them what did they come for. 'On the head of your children,' said they.

'Are they not gone to you along with Aoife?' he said.

'They are not,' they said, 'and Aoife said it was yourself would not let them come.'

It is downhearted and sorrowful Lir was at that news, for he understood well it was Aoife had destroyed or made an end of his children. Early in the morning of the morrow his horses were caught, and he set out on the road to the south-west. When he was as far as the shore of Loch Dairbhreach, the four children saw the horses coming towards them, and it is what Fionnuala said: 'A welcome to the troop of horses I see coming here to the lake; the people they are bringing are strong, there is sadness on them; it is us they are following, it is for us they are looking; let us move over to the shore, Aodh, Fiachra, and comely Conn. Those that are coming can be no others in the world but only Lir and his household.'

Then Lir came to the edge of the lake, and he took notice of the swans having the voice of living people, and he asked them why was it they had that voice. 'I will tell you that, Lir,' said Fionnuala.' 'We are your own four children, that are after being destroyed by your wife, and by the sister of our own mother, through the dint of her jealousy.'

'Is there any way to put you into your own shapes again?' said Lir.

'There is no way,' said Fionnuala, 'for all the men of the world could not help us till we have gone through our time, and that will not be,' she said, 'till the end of nine hundred years.'

When Lir and his people heard that, they gave out three great heavy shouts of grief and sorrow and crying.

'Is there a mind with you,' said Lir, 'to come to us on the land, since you have your own sense and your memory yet?'

'We have not the power,' said Fionnuala, 'to live with any person at all from this time; but we have our own language, the Irish, and we have the power to sing sweet music, and it is enough to satisfy the whole race of men to be listening to that music. And let you stop here tonight,' she said, 'and we will be making music for you.'

So Lir and his people stopped there listening to the music of the swans, and they slept there quietly that night. Lir rose up early on the morning of the morrow and he made this complaint:—

'It is time to go out from this place. I do not sleep though I am in my lying down. To be parted from my dear children, it is that is tormenting my heart.

'It is a bad net I put over you, bringing Aoife, daughter of Oilell of Aran, to the house. I would never have followed that advice if I had known what it would bring upon me.

'O Fionnuala, and the comely Conn, O Aodh, O Fiachra of the beautiful arms; it is not ready I am to go away from you, from the border of the harbour where you are.'

Then Lir went on to the palace of Bodb Dearg, and there was a welcome before him

18

there; and he got a reproach from Bodb Dearg for not bringing his children along with him. 'My grief!' said Lir. 'It is not I that would not bring my children along with me; it was Aoife there beyond, your own foster-child and the sister of their mother, that put them in the shape of four white swans on Loch Dairbhreach, in the sight of the whole of the men of Ireland; but they have their sense with them yet, and their reason, and their voice, and their Irish.'

Bodb Dearg gave a great start when he heard that, and he knew what Lir said was true, and he gave a very sharp reproach to Aoife, and he said: 'This treachery will be worse for yourself in the end, Aoife, than to the children of Lir. And what shape would you yourself think worst of being in?' he said.

'I would think worst of being a witch of the air,' she said.

'It is into that shape I will put you now,' said Bodb, and with that he struck her with a Druid wand, and she was turned into a witch of the air there and then, and she went away on the wind in that shape, and she is in it yet, and will be in it to the end of life and time.

As to Bodb Dearg and the Tuatha de Danaan

they came to the shore of Loch Dairbhreach, and they made their camp there to be listening to the music of the swans. The Sons of the Gael used to be coming no less than the Men of Dea to hear them from every part of Ireland, for there never was any music of any delight heard in Ireland to compare with that music of the swans. They used to be telling stories, and to be talking with the men of Ireland every day, and with their teachers and their fellow-pupils and their friends. Every night they used to sing very sweet music of the Sidhe; and every one that heard that music would sleep sound and quiet what ever trouble or long sickness might be on him; for every one that heard the music of the birds, it is happy and contented he would be after it.

These two gatherings now of the Tuatha de Danaan and of the Sons of the Gael stopped there around Loch Dairbhreach through the length of three hundred years. And it is then Fionnuala said to her brothers: 'Do you know,' she said, 'we have spent all we have to spend of our time here, but this one night only.'

And there was great sorrow on the sons of Lir when they heard that, for they thought it the same as to be living people again, to be talking with their friends and their companions on Loch Dairbhreach, in comparison with going on the cold, fretful sea of the Maoil in the north. They came early on the morrow to speak with their father and with their foster-father, and they bade them farewell, and Fionnuala made this complaint:—

'Farewell to you, Bodb Dearg, the man with whom all knowledge is in pledge. And farewell to our father along with you, Lir of the Hill of the White Field.

'The time is come, as I think, for us to part from you, O pleasant company; my grief it is not on a visit we are going to you.

'From this day out, O friends of our heart, our comrades, it is on the tormented course of the Maoil we will be, without the voice of any person near us.

'Three hundred years there, and three hundred years in the bay of the men of Domnann, it is a pity for the four comely children of Lir, the salt waves of the sea to be their covering by night.

'O three brothers, with the ruddy faces gone from you, let them all leave the lake now, the great troop that loved us, it is sorrowful our parting is.'

After that complaint they took to flight, lightly, airily, till they came to Sruth na Maoile between Ireland and Alban. That was a grief to the men of Ireland, and they gave out an order no swan was to be killed from that out, what ever chance there might be of killing one, all through Ireland.

It was a bad dwelling-place for the children of Lir they to be on Sruth na Maoile. When they saw the wide coast about them, they were filled with cold and with sorrow, and they thought nothing of all they had gone through before, in comparison to what they were going through on that sea.

Now one night while they were there a great storm came on them, and it is what Fionnuala said: 'My dear brothers,' she said, 'it is a pity for us not to be making ready for this night, for it is certain the storm will separate us from one another. And let us,' she said, 'settle on some place where we can meet afterwards, if we are driven from one another in the night.'

'Let us settle,' said the others, 'to meet one another at Carraig na Ron, the Rock of the Seals, for we all have knowledge of it.'

When midnight came, the wind came on them with it, and the noise of the waves

increased, and the lightning was flashing, and a rough storm came sweeping down, the way the children of Lir were scattered over the great sea, and the wideness of it set them astray, so that no one of them could know what way the others went. But after that storm a great quiet came on the sea, and Fionnuala was alone on Sruth na Maoile; and when she took notice that her brothers were wanting she was lamenting after them greatly, and she made this complaint:—

'It is a pity for me to be alive in the state I am; it is frozen to my sides my wings are; it is little that the wind has not broken my heart in my body, with the loss of Aodh.

'To be three hundred years on Loch Dairbhreach without going into my own shape, it is worse to me the time I am on Sruth na Maoile.

'The three I loved, Och! the three I loved, that slept under the shelter of my feathers; till the dead come back to the living I will see them no more for ever.

'It is a pity I to stay after Fiachra, and after Aodh, and after comely Conn, and with no account of them; my grief I to be here to face every hardship this night.'

She stopped all night there upon the Rock of the Seals until the rising of the sun, looking out

over the sea on every side till at last she saw
Conn coming to her, his feathers wet through
and his head hanging, and her heart gave him a
great welcome; and then Fiachra came wet and
perished and worn out, and he could not say a
word they could understand with the dint of the
cold and the hardship he had gone through.
Fionnuala put him under her wings, and she
said: 'We would be well off now if Aodh would
but come to us.'

It was not long after that, they saw Aodh
coming, his head dry and his feathers beautiful,
and Fionnuala gave him a great welcome, and
she put him under the feathers of her breast,
and Fiachra under her right wing and Conn
under her left wing, the way she could put her
feathers over them all. 'And Och! my brothers,'
she said, 'this was a bad night to us, and it is
many of its like are before us from this out.'

They stayed a long time after that, suffering
cold and misery on the Maoil, till at last a night
came on them they had never known the like of
before, for frost and snow and wind and cold.
They were crying and lamenting the hardship of
their life, and the cold of the night and the
greatness of the snow and the hardness of the
wind, and after they had suffered cold to the

end of a year, a worse night again came on them, in the middle of winter. They were on Carraig na Ron, and the water froze about them, and as they rested on the rock, their feet and their wings and their feathers froze to the rock, the way they were not able to move from it. They made such a hard struggle to get away, that they left the skin of their feet and their feathers and the tops of their wings on the rock after them.

'My grief, children of Lir,' said Fionnuala, 'it is bad our state is now, for we cannot bear the salt water to touch us, and there are bonds on us not to leave it; and if the salt water goes into our sores,' she said, 'we will get our death.'

And she made this complaint:—

'It is keening we are tonight; without feathers to cover our bodies; it is cold the rough, uneven rocks are under our bare feet.

'It is bad our stepmother was to us the time she played enchantments on us, sending us out like swans upon the sea.

'Our washing place is on the ridge of the bay, in the foam of flying manes of the sea; our share of the ale feast is the salt water of the blue tide.

'One daughter and three sons; it is in the clefts of the rocks we are; it is on the hard rocks we are, it is a pity the way we are.'

However, they came on to the course of the Maoil again, and the salt water was sharp and rough and bitter to them, but if it was itself, they were not able to avoid it or to get shelter from it. And they were there by the shore under that hardship till such time as their feathers grew again, and their wings, and till their sores were entirely healed. Then they used to go every day to the shore of Ireland or of Alban, but they had to come back to Sruth na Maoile every night.

Now they came one day to the mouth of the Banna, to the north of Ireland, and they saw a troop of riders, beautiful, of the one colour, with well-trained pure white horses under them, and they travelling the road straight from the south-west.

'Do you know who those riders are, sons of Lir?' said Fionnuala.

'We do not,' they said, 'but it is likely they might be some troop of the Sons of the Gael, or of the Tuatha de Danaan.'

They moved over closer to the shore then, that they might know who they were, and when the riders saw them they came to meet them until they were able to hold talk together.

27

The chief men among them were two sons of Bodb Dearg, Aodh Aithfhiosach, of the quick wits, and Fergus Fithchiollach, of the chess, and a third part of the Riders of the Sidhe along with them, and it was for the swans they had been looking for a long while before that, and when they came together they wished one another a kind and loving welcome.

And the children of Lir asked for news of all the Men of Dea, and above all of Lir, and Bodb Dearg and their people.

'They are well, and they are in the one place together,' said they, 'in your father's house at Sidhe Fionnachaidh, using the Feast of Age pleasantly and happily, and with no uneasiness on them, only for being without yourselves, and without knowledge of what happened to you from the day you left Loch Dairbhreach.'

'That has not been the way with us,' said Fionnuala, 'for we have gone through great hardship and uneasiness and misery on the tides of the sea until this day.'

And she made this complaint:—

'There is delight tonight with the household of Lir! Plenty of ale with them and of wine, although it is in a cold dwelling-place this night are the four children of the king.

'It is without a spot our bedclothes are, our bodies covered over with curved feathers; but it is often we were dressed in purple, and we drinking pleasant mead.

'It is what our food is and our drink, the white sand and the bitter water of the sea; it is often we drank mead of hazel-nuts from round four-lipped drinking cups.

'It is what our beds are, bare rocks out of the power of the waves; it is often there used to be spread out for us beds of the breast-feathers of birds.

'Though it is our work now to be swimming through the frost and through the noise of the waves, it is often a company of the sons of kings were riding after us to the Hill of Bodb.

'It is what wasted my strength, to be going and coming over the current of the Maoil the way I never was used to, and never to be in the sunshine on the soft grass.

'Fiachra's bed and Conn's bed is to come under the cover of my wings on the sea. Aodh has his place under the feathers of my breast, the four of us side by side.

'The teaching of Manannan without deceit, the talk of Bodb Dearg on the pleasant ridge; the voice of Angus, his sweet kisses; it is by their side I used to be without grief.'

After that the riders went on to Lir's house, and they told the chief men of the Tuatha de Danaan all the birds had gone through, and the state they were in. 'We have no power over them,' the chief men said, 'but we are glad they are living yet, for they will get help in the end of time.'

As to the children of Lir, they went back towards their old place in the Maoil, and they stopped there till the time they had to spend on it was spent. And then Fionnuala said: 'The time is come for us to leave this place. And it is to Irrus Domnann we must go now,' she said, 'after our three hundred years here. And indeed there will be no rest for us there, or any standing ground, or any shelter from the storms. But since it is time for us to go, let us set out on the cold wind, the way we will not go astray.'

So they set out in that way, and left Sruth na Maoile behind them, and went to the point of Irrus Domnann, and there they stopped, and it is a life of misery and a cold life they led there. One time the sea froze about them that they could not move at all, and the brothers were lamenting, and Fionnuala was comforting them, for she knew help would come to them in the end.

They stayed at Irrus Domnann till the time they had to spend there was spent. And then Fionnuala said: 'The time is come for us to go back to Sidhe Fionnachaidh, where our father is with his household and with all our own people.'

'It pleases us to hear that,' they said.

So they set out flying through the air lightly till they came to Sidhe Fionnachaidh; and it is how they found the place, empty before them, and nothing in it but green hillocks and thickets of nettles, without a house, without a fire, without a hearthstone. And the four pressed close to one another then, and they gave out three sorrowful cries, and Fionnuala made this complaint:—

'It is a wonder to me this place is, and it without a house, without a dwelling-place. To see it the way it is now, Ochone! it is bitterness to my heart.

'Without dogs, without hounds for hunting, without women, without great kings; we never knew it to be like this when our father was in it.

'Without horns, without cups, without drinking in the lighted house; without young men, without riders; the way it is tonight is a foretelling of sorrow.

'The people of the place to be as they are now, Ochone! it is grief to my heart! It is plain to my mind tonight the lord of the house is not living.

'Och, house where we used to see music and playing and the gathering of people! I think it a great change to see it lonely the way it is tonight.

'The greatness of the hardships we have gone through going from one wave to another of the sea, we never heard of the like of them coming on any other person.

'It is seldom this place had its part with grass and bushes; the man is not living that would know us, it would be a wonder to him to see us here.'

However, the children of Lir stopped that night in their father's place and their grandfather's, where they had been reared, and they were singing very sweet music of the Sidhe. They rose up early on the morning of the morrow and went to Inis Gluaire, and all the birds of the country gathered near them on Loch na nEan, the Lake of the Birds. They used to go out to feed every day to the far parts of the country, to Inis Geadh and to Accuill, the place

Donn, son of Miled, and his people that were drowned were buried, and to all the western islands of Connacht, and they used to go back to Inis Gluaire every night.

It was about that time it happened them to meet with a young man of good race, and his name was Aibric; and he often took notice of the birds, and their singing was sweet to him and he loved them greatly, and they loved him. It is this young man that told the whole story of all that had happened them, and put it in order.

And the story he told of what happened them in the end is this.

It was after the faith of Christ and blessed Patrick came into Ireland, that Saint Mochaomhog came to Inis Gluaire. The first night he came to the island, the children of Lir heard the voice of his bell, ringing near them, and the brothers started up with fright when they heard it. 'We do not know,' they said, 'what is that weak, unpleasing voice we hear.'

'That is the voice of the bell of Mochaomhog,' said Fionnuala, 'and it is through that bell,' she said, 'you will be set free from pain and from misery.'

They listened to that music of the bell till the matins were done, and then they began to sing the low, sweet music of the Sidhe.

Mochaomhog was listening to them, and he prayed to God to show him who was singing that music, and it was shown to him that the children of Lir were singing it. On the morning of the morrow he went forward to the Lake of the Birds, and he saw the swans before him on the lake, and he went down to them at the brink of the shore. 'Are you the children of Lir?' he said.

'We are indeed,' said they.

'I give thanks to God for that,' said he, 'for it is for your sakes I am come to this island beyond any other island, and let you come to land now,' he said, 'and give your trust to me, that you may do good deeds and part from your sins.'

They came to the land after that, and they put trust in Mochaomhog, and he brought them to his own dwelling place, and they used to be hearing Mass with him. And he got a good smith and bade him make chains of bright silver for them, and he put a chain between Aodh and Fionnuala, and a chain between Conn and Fiachra. The four of them were raising his heart and gladdening his mind, and no danger and no distress that was on the swans before put any trouble on them now.

Now the king of Connacht at that time was Lairgnen, son of Colman, son of Cobthach, and Deoch, daugher of Finghin, was his wife. That was the coming together of the Man from the North and the Woman from the South, that Aoife had spoken of.

The woman heard talk of the birds, and a great desire came on her to get them, and she bade Lairgnen to bring them to her, and he said he would ask them of Mochaomhog.

She gave her word she would not stop another night with him unless he would bring them to her, and she set out from the house there and then. Lairgnen sent messengers after her to bring her back, and they did not overtake her till she was at Cill Dun. She went back home with them then, and Lairgnen sent messengers to ask the birds of Mochaomhog, and he did not get them.

There was great anger on Lairgnen then, and he went himself to the place Mochaomhog was, and he asked was it true he had refused him the birds. 'It is true indeed,' said he. At that Lairgnen rose up, and he took hold of the swans, and pulled them off the altar, two birds in each hand, to bring them away to Deoch. But no sooner had he laid his hand on them than their bird skins fell off, and what was in their place was three lean, withered old men and a thin withered old woman, without blood or flesh.

Lairgnen gave a great start at that, and he went out from the place. It is then Fionnuala said to Mochaomhog: 'Come and baptise us now, for it is short till our death comes; and it is certain you do not think worse of parting with us than we do of parting with you. And make our grave afterwards,' she said, 'and lay Conn at my right side and Fiachra on my left side, and Aodh before my face, between my two arms. And pray to the God of Heaven,' she said, 'that you may be able to baptise us.'

The children of Lir were baptised then, and they died and were buried as Fionnuala had desired; Fiachra and Conn one at each side of her, and Aodh before her face. A stone was put

over them, and their names were written in Ogham, and they were keened there, and heaven was gained for their souls.

And that is the fate of the children of Lir so far.

2

The Coming of Finn

At the time Finn was born his father Cumhal, of the sons of Baiscne, Head of the Fianna of Ireland, had been killed in battle by the sons of Morna that were fighting with him for the leadership. And his mother, that was beautiful long-haired Muirne, daughter of Tadg, son of Nuada of the Tuatha de Danaan and of Ethlinn, mother of Lugh of the Long Hand, did not dare to keep him with her; and two women, Bodhmall, the woman Druid, and Liath Luachra, came and brought him away to care for him.

It was to the woods of Slieve Bladhma they brought him, and they nursed him secretly, because of his father's enemies, the sons of Morna, and they kept him there a long time.

And Muirne, his mother, took another husband that was king of Carraighe; but at the end of six years she came to see Finn, going through every lonely place till she came to the wood, and there she found the little hunting cabin, and the boy asleep in it, and she lifted him up in her arms and kissed him, and she sang a little sleepy song to him; and then she said farewell to the women, and she went away again.

And the two women went on caring for him till he came to sensible years; and one day when he went out he saw a wild duck on the lake with her clutch, and he made a cast at her that cut the wings off her that she could not fly, and he brought her back to the cabin, and that was his first hunt.

And they gave him good training in running and leaping and swimming. One of them would run round a tree, and she having a thorn switch, and Finn after her with another switch, and each one trying to hit at the other; and they would leave him in a field, and hares along with him, and would bid him not to let the hares quit the field, but to keep before them which ever way they would go; and to teach him swimming they would throw him into the water and let him make his way out.

But after a while he went away with a troop of poets, to hide from the sons of Morna, and they hid him in the mountain of Crotta Cliach;

but there was a robber in Leinster at that time, Fiacuil, son of Codhna, and he came where the poets were in Fidh Gaible and killed them all. But he spared the child and brought him to his own house, that was in a cold marsh. But the two women, Bodhmall and Liath, came looking for him after a while, and Fiacuil gave him up to them, and they brought him back to the same place he was before.

He grew up there, straight and strong and fair-haired and beautiful. And one day he was out in Slieve Bladhma, and the two women along with him, and they saw before them a herd of wild deer of the mountain. 'It is a pity,' said the old women, 'not to be able to get a deer of those deer.'

'I will get one for you,' said Finn; and with that he followed after them, and caught two stags of them and brought them home to the hunting cabin. And after that he used to be hunting for them every day. But at last they said to him: 'It is best for you to leave us now, for the sons of Morna are watching again to kill you.'

So he went away then by himself, and never stopped till he came to Magh Lifé, and there he saw young lads swimming in a lake, and they called to him to swim against them. So he went into the lake, and he beat them at swimming. 'Fair he is and well shaped,' they said when they saw him swimming, and it was from that time he got the name of Finn, that is, Fair. But they got to be jealous of his strength, and he went away and left them .

He went on then till he came to Loch Lein, and he took service there with the King of Finntraigh; and there was no hunter like him, and the king said: 'If Cumhal had left a son, you would be that son.'

He went from that king after, and he went into Carraighe, and there he took service with the king, that had taken his mother Muirne for his wife. And one day they were playing chess together, and he won seven games one after another. 'Who are you at all?' said the king then.

'I am a son of a countryman of the Luigne of Teamhair,' said Finn.

'That is not so,' said the king, 'but you are the son that Muirne my wife bore to Cumhal. And do not stop here any longer,' he said, 'that you may not be killed under my protection.'

From that he went into Connacht looking for his father's brother, Crimall, son of Trenmor;

and as he was going on his way he heard the crying of a lone woman. He went to her, and
looked at her, and tears of blood were on her
face. 'Your face is red with blood, woman,' he
said.

'I have reason for it,' said she, 'for my only
son is after being killed by a great fighting man
that came on us.'

Finn followed after the big champion and
fought with him and killed him. And the man
he killed was the same man that had given
Cumhal his first wound in the battle where he
got his death, and had brought away his
treasure-bag with him.

Now as to that treasure-bag, it is of a crane
skin it was made, that was one time the skin of
Aoife, the beautiful sweetheart of Ilbrec, son of
Manannan, that was put into the shape of a
crane through jealousy. And it was in Manannan's house it used to be, and there were
treasures kept in it, Manannan's shirt and his
knife, and the belt and the smith's hook of
Goibniu, and the shears of the King of Alban,
and the helmet of the King of Lochlann, and a
belt of the skin of a great fish, and the bones of
Asal's pig that had been brought to Ireland by
the sons of Tuireann. All those treasures would

be in the bag at full tide, but at the ebbing of the tide it would be empty. And it went from Manannan to Lugh, son of Ethlinn, and after that to Cumhal, that was husband to Muirne, Ethlinn's daughter.

And Finn took the bag and brought it with him till he found Crimall, that was now an old man, living in a lonely place, and some of the old men of the Fianna were with him, and used to go hunting for him. And Finn gave him the bag, and told him his whole story.

And then he said farewell to Crimall, and went on to learn poetry from Finegas, a poet that was living at the Boinn, for the poets thought it was always on the brink of water poetry was revealed to them. And he did not give him his own name, but he took the name of Deimne. Seven years, now, Finegas had stopped at the Boinn, watching the salmon, for it was in the prophecy that he would eat the salmon of knowledge that would come there, and that he would have all knowledge after. And when at the last the salmon of knowledge came, he brought it to where Finn was, and bade him to roast it, but he bade him not to eat any of it. And when Finn brought him the salmon after a while he said: 'Did you eat any of it at all, boy?'

'I did not,' said Finn, 'but I burned my thumb putting down a blister that rose on the skin, and after doing that, I put my thumb in my mouth.'

'What is your name, boy?' said Finegas.

'Deimne,' said he.

'It is not, but it is Finn your name is, and it is to you and not to myself the salmon was given in the prophecy.'

With that he gave Finn the whole of the salmon, and from that time Finn had the knowledge that came from the nuts of the nine hazels of wisdom that grow beside the well that is below the sea.

And besides the wisdom he got then, there was a second wisdom came to him another time, and this is the way it happened.

There was a well of the moon belonging to Beag, son of Buan, of the Tuatha de Danaan, and whoever would drink out of it would get wisdom, and after a second drink he would get the gift of foretelling. And the three daughters of Beag, son of Buan, had charge of the well, and they would not part with a vessel of it for anything less than red gold. And one day Finn chanced to be hunting in the rushes near the

well, and the three women ran out to hinder him from coming to it, and one of them that had a vessel of the water in her hand, threw it at him to stop him, and a share of the water went into his mouth. And from that out he had all the knowledge that the water of that well could give.

And he learned the three ways of poetry; and this is the poem he made to show he had got his learning well:—

'It is the month of May is the pleasant time: its face is beautiful: the blackbird sings his full song, the living wood is his holding, the cuckoos are singing and ever singing; there is a welcome before the brightness of the summer.

'Summer is lessening the rivers, the swift horses are looking for the pool; the heath spreads out its long hair, the weak white bog-down grows. A wildness comes on the heart of the deer; the sad restless sea is asleep.

'Bees with their little strength carry a load reaped from the flowers; the cattle go up muddy to the mountains; the ant has a good full feast.

'The harp of the woods is playing music; there is colour on the hills, and a haze on the full

46

lakes, and entire peace upon every sail.

'The corncrake is speaking, a loud-voiced poet; the high lonely waterfall is singing a welcome to the warm pool, the talking of the rushes has begun.

'The light swallows are darting; the loudness of music is around the hill; the fat soft mast is budding; there is grass on the trembling bogs.

'The bog is as dark as the feathers of the raven; the cuckoo makes a loud welcome; the speckled salmon is leaping; as strong is the leaping of the swift fighting man.

'The man is gaining; the girl is in her comely growing power; every wood is without fault from the top to the ground, and every wide good plain.

'It is pleasant is the colour of the time; rough winter is gone; every plentiful wood is white; summer is a joyful peace.

'A flock of birds pitches in the meadow; there are sounds in the green fields, there is in them a clear rushing stream.

'There is a hot desire on you for the racing of horses; twisted holly makes a leash for the hound; a bright spear has been shot into the earth, and the flag-flower is golden under it.

'A weak lasting little bird is singing at the top

of his voice; the lark is singing clear tidings; May without fault, of beautiful colours.

'I have another story for you; the ox is lowing, the winter is creeping in, the summer is gone. High and cold the wind, low the sun, cries are about us; the sea is quarrelling.

'The ferns are reddened and their shape is hidden; the cry of the wild goose is heard; the cold has caught the wings of the birds; it is the time of ice-frost, hard, unhappy.'

And after that, Finn being but a young lad yet, made himself ready and went up at Samhain time to the gathering of the High King at Teamhair. And it was the law at that gathering, no one to raise a quarrel or bring out any grudge against another through the whole of the time it lasted. And the king and his chief men, and Goll, son of Morna, that was now Head of the Fianna, and Caoilte, son of Ronan, and Conan, son of Morna, of the sharp words, were sitting at a feast in the great house of the Middle Court; and the young lad came in and took his place among them, and none of them knew who he was. The High King looked at him then, and the

49

horn of meetings was brought to him, and he put it into the boy's hand, and asked him who was he.

'I am Finn, son of Cumhal,' he said, 'son of the man that used to be head over the Fianna, and king of Ireland; and I am come now to get your friendship, and to give you my service.'

'You are son of a friend, boy,' said the king, 'and son of a man I trusted.'

Then Finn rose up and made his agreement of service and of faithfulness to the king; and the king took him by the hand and put him sitting beside his own son, and they gave themselves to drinking and to pleasure for a while.

Every year, now, at Samhain time, for nine years there had come a man of the Tuatha de Danaan out of Sidhe Finnachaidh in the north, and had burned up Teamhair. Aillen, son of Midhna, his name was, and it is the way he used to come playing music of the Sidhe, and all the people that heard it would fall asleep. And when they were all in their sleep, he would let a flame of fire out of his mouth, and would blow the flame till all Teamhair was burned.

The king rose up at the feast after a while, and his smooth horn in his hand, and it is what he said: 'If I could find among you, men of Ireland, any man that would keep Teamhair till the break of day tomorrow without being burned by Aillen, son of Midhna, I would give him whatever inheritance is right for him to have, whether it be much or little.'

But the men of Ireland made no answer, for they knew well that at the sound of the sweet pitiful music made by that comely man of the Sidhe, even women in their pains and men that were wounded would fall asleep.

It is then Finn rose up and spoke to the King of Ireland. 'Who will be your sureties that you will fulfil this?' he said.

'The kings of the provinces of Ireland,' said the king, 'and Cithruadh with his Druids.'

So they gave their pledges, and Finn took in hand to keep Teamhair safe till the breaking of day on the morrow.

Now there was a fighting man among the followers of the King of Ireland, Fiacha, son of Conga, that Cumhal, Finn's father, used to have a great liking for, and he said to Finn: 'Well, boy,' he said, 'what reward would you give me if I would bring you a deadly spear, that no false cast was ever made with?'

'What reward are you asking of me?' said Finn.

'Whatever your right hand wins at any time, the third of it to be mine,' said Fiacha, 'and a third of your trust and your friendship to be mine.'

'I will give you that,' said Finn.

Then Fiacha brought him the spear, unknown to the sons of Morna or to any other person, and he said: 'When you will hear the music of the Sidhe, let you strip the covering off the head of the spear and put it to your forehead, and the power of the spear will not let sleep come upon you.'

Then Finn rose up before all the men of Ireland, and he made a round of the whole of Teamhair. And it was not long till he heard the sorrowful music, and he stripped the covering from the head of the spear, and he held the power of it to his forehead. And Aillen went on playing his little harp, till he had put every one in their sleep as he was used; and then he let a flame of fire out from his mouth to burn Teamhair. And Finn held up his fringed crimson cloak against the flame, and it fell down through the air and went into the ground, bringing the four-folded cloak with it deep into the earth.

And when Aillen saw his spells were

destroyed, he went back to Sidhe Finnachaidh on the top of Slieve Fuad; but Finn followed after him there, and as Aillen was going in at the door he made a cast of the spear that went through his heart. And he struck his head off then, and brought it back to Teamhair, and fixed it on a crooked pole and left it there till the rising of the sun over the heights and invers of the country.

And Aillen's mother came to where his body was lying, and there was great grief on her, and she made this compaint:—

'Ochone! Aillen is fallen, chief of the Sidhe of Beinn Boirche; the slow clouds of death are come on him. Och! he was pleasant, Och! he was kind. Aillen, son of Midhna of Slieve Fuad.

'Nine times he burned Teamhair. It is a great name he was always looking for, Ochone, Ochone, Aillen!'

And at the breaking of day, the king and all the men of Ireland came out upon the town at Teamhair where Finn was.

'King,' said Finn, 'there is the head of the man that burned Teamhair, and the pipe and the harp that made his music. And it is what I think,' he said, 'that Teamhair and all that is in it is saved.'

Then they all came together into the place of counsel, and it is what they agreed, the head-ship of the Fianna of Ireland to be given to Finn. And the king said to Goll, son of Morna: 'Well, Goll,' he said, 'is it your choice to quit Ireland or to put your hand in Finn's hand?'

'By my word, I will give Finn my hand,' said Goll.

And when the charms that used to bring good luck had done their work, the chief men of the Fianna rose up and struck their hands in Finn's hand, and Goll, son of Morna, was the first to give him his hand the way there would be less shame on the rest for doing it.

And Finn kept the headship of the Fianna until the end; and the place he lived in was Almhuin of Leinster, where the white dun was made by Nuada of the Tuatha de Danaan, that was as white as if all the lime in Ireland was put on it, and that got its name from the great herd of cattle that died fighting one time around the well, and that left their horns there, speckled horns and white.

And as to Finn himself, he was a king and a seer and a poet; a Druid and a knowledgeable man; and everything he said was sweet-sound-ing to his people. And a better fighting man than Finn never struck his hand into a king's hand, and whatever any one ever said of him, he was three times better. And of his justice it used to be said, that if his enemy and his own son had come before him to be judged, it is fair judgment he would have given between them. And as to his generosity it used to be said, he never denied any man as long as he had a mouth to eat with, and legs to bring away what he gave him; and he left no woman without her bride-price, and no man without his pay; and he never promised at night what he would not fulfil on the morrow, and he never promised in the day what he would not fulfil at night, and he never forsook his right-hand friend. And if he was quiet in peace he was angry in battle, and Oisin his son and Osgar his son's son followed him in that. There was a young man of Ulster came and claimed kinship with them one time, saying they were of the one blood. 'If that is so,' said Oisin, 'it is from the men of Ulster we took the madness and the angry heart we have in battle.'

'That is so indeed,' said Finn.

3

Finn's Household

The number of the Fianna of Ireland at that time was seven score and ten chief men, every one of them having three times nine fighting men under him. And every man of them was bound to three things, to take no cattle by oppression, not to refuse any man, as to cattle or riches; no one of them to fall back before nine fighting men. And there was no man taken into the Fianna until his tribe and his kindred would give securities for him, that even if they themselves were all killed he would not look for satisfaction for their death. But if he himself would harm others, that harm was not to be avenged on his people. And there was no man taken into the Fianna till he knew the twelve books of poetry. And before any man was taken, he would be put into a deep hole in the ground up to his middle, and he having his shield and a hazel rod in his hand. And nine men would go the length of ten furrows from him and would cast their spears at him at the one time. And if he got a wound from one of them, he was not thought fit to join with the Fianna. And after that again, his hair would be fastened up, and he put to run through the woods of Ireland, and the Fianna following after him to try could they wound him, and only the length of a branch between themselves and himself when they started. And if they came up with him and wounded him, he was not let join them; or if his spears had trembled in his hand, or if a branch of a tree had undone the plaiting of his hair, or if he had cracked a dry stick under his foot, and he running. And they would not take him among them till he had made a leap over a stick the height of himself, and till he had stooped under one the height of his knee, and till he had taken a thorn out from his foot with his nail, and he running his fastest. But if he had done all these things, he was of Finn's people.

It was good wages Finn and the Fianna got at that time; in every district a townland, in every house the fostering of a pup or a whelp from Samhain to Beltaine, and a great many things along with that. But good as the pay was, the hardships and the dangers they went through for it were greater. For they had to hinder the strangers and robbers from beyond the seas, and every bad thing, from coming into Ireland. And they had hard work enough in doing that.

And besides the fighting men, Finn had with him his five Druids, the best that ever came into the west, Cainnelsciath, of the Shining Shield, one of them was, that used to bring down knowledge from the clouds in the sky before Finn, and that could foretell battles. And he had his five wonderful physicians, four of them belonging to Ireland, and one that came over the sea from the east. And he had his five high poets and his twelve musicians, that had among them Daighre, son of Morna, and Suanach, son of Senshenn, that was Finn's teller of old stories, the sweetest that ever took a harp in his hand in Ireland or in Alban. And he had his three cup-bearers and his six door-keepers and his horn-players and the stewards of his house and his huntsman, Comhrag of the five hundred hounds, and his serving-men that were under Garbhcronan, of the Rough Buzzing; and a great troop of others along with them.

And there were fifty of the best sewing-women in Ireland brought together in a rath on Magh Feman, under the charge of a daugher of the King of Britain, and they used to be making clothing for the Fianna through the whole of the year. And three of them, that were a king's daughters, used to be making music for the rest on a little silver harp; and there was a very great candlestick of stone in the middle of the rath, for they were not willing to kindle a fire more than three times in the year for fear the smoke and the ashes might harm the needlework.

And of all his musicians the one Finn thought most of was Cnu Deireoil, the Little Nut, that came to him from the Sidhe.

It was at Slieve-na-mban, for hunting, Finn was the time he came to him. Sitting down he was on the turf-built grave that is there; and when he looked around him he saw a small little man about four feet in height standing on the grass. Light yellow hair he had, hanging down to his waist, and he playing music on his harp. And the music he was making had no fault in it at all, and it is much that the whole of the Fianna did not fall asleep with the sweetness of its sound. He came up then, and put his hand in Finn's hand. 'Where do you come from, little one, yourself and your sweet music?' said Finn.

'I am come,' he said, 'out of the place of the Sidhe in Slieve-na-mban, where ale is drunk and made; and it is to be in your company for a while I am come here.'

'You will get good rewards from me, and riches and red gold,' said Finn, 'and my full friendship, for I like you well.'

'That is the best luck ever came to you, Finn,' said all the rest of the Fianna, for they were well pleased to have him in their company. And they gave him the name of the Little Nut; and he was good in speaking, and he had so good a memory he never forgot anything he had heard east or west; and there was no one but must listen to his music, and all the Fianna liked him well. And there were some said he was a son of Lugh Lamh-Fada, of the Long Hand.

And the five musicians of the Fianna were brought to him, to learn the music of the Sidhe he had brought from that other place; for there was never any music heard on earth but his was better. These were the three best things Finn ever got, Bran and Sceolan that were without fault, and the Little Nut from the House of the Sidhe in Slieve-na-mban.

4

Birth of Bran

This, now, is the story of the birth of Bran.

Finn's mother, Muirne, came one time to Almhuin, and she brought with her Tuiren, her sister. And Iollan Eachtach, a chief man of the Fianna of Ulster, was at Almhuin at the time, and he gave his love to Tuiren, and asked her in marriage, and brought her to his own house. But before they went, Finn made him give his word he would bring her back safe and sound if ever he asked for her, and he bade him find sureties for himself among the chief men of the Fianna. And Iollan did that, and the sureties he got were Caoilte and Goll and Lugaidh Lamha, and it was Lugaidh gave her into the hand of Iollan Eachtach.

But before Iollan made that marriage, he had a sweetheart of the Sidhe, Uchtdealb of the Fair Breast; and there came great jealousy on her when she knew he had taken a wife. And she took the appearance of Finn's woman-messenger, and she came to the house where Tuiren was, and she said: 'Finn sends health and long life to you, queen, and he bids you to make a great feast; and come with me now,' she said, 'till I speak a few words with you, for there is hurry on me.'

So Tuiren went out with her, and when they were away from the house the woman of the Sidhe took out her dark Druid rod from under her cloak and gave her a blow of it that changed her into a hound, the most beautiful that was ever seen. And then she went on, bringing the hound with her, to the house of Fergus Fionnliath, king of the harbour of Gallimh. And it is the way Fergus was, he was the most unfriendly man to dogs in the whole world, and he would not let one stop in the same house with him. But it is what Uchtdealb said to him: 'Finn wishes you life and health, Fergus, and he says to you to take good care of his hound till he comes himself; and mind her well,' she said, 'for she is with young, and do not let her go hunting when her time is near, or Finn will be no way thankful to you.'

'I wonder at that message,' said Fergus, 'for Finn knows well there is not in the world a man has less liking for dogs than myself. But for all that,' he said, 'I will not refuse Finn the first time he sent a hound to me.'

And when he brought the hound out to try her, she was the best he ever knew, and she never saw the wild creature she would not run down; and Fergus took a great liking for hounds from that out.

And when her time came near, they did not let her go hunting any more, and she gave birth to two whelps.

And as to Finn, when he heard his mother's sister was not living with Iollan Eachtach, he called to him for the fulfilment of the pledge that was given to the Fianna. And Iollan asked time to go looking for Tuiren, and he gave his word that if he did not find her, he would give himself up in satisfaction for her. So they agreed to that, and Iollan went to the hill where Uchtdealb was, his sweetheart of the Sidhe, and told her the way things were with him, and the promise he had made to give himself up to the Fianna.

'If that is so,' said she, 'and if you will give me your pledge to keep me as your sweetheart to the end of your life. I will free you from that danger.'

So Iollan gave her his promise, and she went

to the house of Fergus Fionnliath, and she brought Tuiren away and put her own shape on her again, and gave her up to Finn. And Finn gave her to Lugaidh Lamha that asked her in marriage.

And as to the two whelps, they stopped always with Finn, and the names he gave them were Bran and Sceolan.

5

Oisin's Mother

It happened one time Finn and his men were coming back from the hunting, a beautiful fawn started up before them, and they followed after it, men and dogs, till at last they were all tired and fell back, all but Finn himself and Bran and Sceolan. And suddenly as they were going through a valley, the fawn stopped and lay down on the smooth grass, and Bran and Sceolan came up with it, and they did not harm it at all, but went playing about it, licking its neck and its face.

There was wonder on Finn when he saw that, and he went on home to Almhuin, and the fawn followed after him playing with the hounds, and it came with them into the house at Almhuin. And when Finn was alone later that evening, a beautiful young woman having a rich dress came before him, and she told him it was she herself was the fawn he was after hunting that day. 'And it is for refusing the love of Fear

Doirche, the Dark Druid of the Men of Dea,' she said, 'I was put in this shape. And through the length of three years,' she said, 'I have lived the life of a wild deer in a far part of Ireland, and I am hunted like a wild deer. And a serving-man of the Dark Druid took pity on me,' she said, 'and he said that if I was once within the dun of the Fianna of Ireland, the Druid would have no more power over me. So I made away, and I never stopped through the whole length of a day till I came into the district of Almhuin. And I never stopped then till there was no one after me but only Bran and Sceolan, that have human wits; and I was safe with them, for they knew my nature to be like their own.'

Then Finn gave her his love, and took her as his wife, and she stopped in Almhuin. And so great was his love for her, he gave up his hunting and all the things he used to take pleasure in, and gave his mind to no other thing but herself.

But at last the men of Lochlann came against Ireland, and their ships were in the bay below Beinn Edair, and they landed there.

And Finn and the battalions of the Fianna went out against them, and drove them back. And at the end of seven days Finn came back home, and he went quickly over the plain of

Almhuin, thinking to see Sadbh his wife looking out from the dun, but there was no sign of
her. And when he came to the dun, all his
people came out to meet him, but they had a
very downcast look.

'Where is the flower of Almhuin, beautiful
gentle Sadbh?' he asked them.

And it is what they said: 'While you were
away fighting, your likeness, and the likeness of
Bran and Sceolan appeared before the dun, and
we thought we heard the sweet call of the Dord
Fiann. And Sadbh, that was so good and so
beautiful, came out of the house,' they said,
'and she went out of the gates, and she would
not listen to us, and we could not stop her.

'"Let me go meet my love," she said, "my
husband, the father of the child that is not
born."

'And with that she went running out towards
the shadow of yourself that was before her, and
that had its arms stretched out to her. But no
sooner did she touch it than she gave a great cry,
and the shadow lifted up a hazel rod, and on the
moment it was a fawn was standing on the
grass. Three times she turned and made for the
gate of the dun, but the two hounds the shadow
had with him went after her and took her by the

throat and dragged her back to him. And by your hand of valor, Finn,' they said, 'we ourselves made no delay till we went out on the plain after her. But it is our grief, they had all vanished, and there was not to be seen woman, or fawn or Druid, but we could hear the quick tread of feet on the hard plain, and the howling of dogs. And if you would ask every one of us in what quarter he heard those sounds, he would tell you a different one.'

When Finn heard that, he said no word at all, but he struck his breast over and over again with his shut hands. And he went then to his own inside room, and his people saw him no more for that day, or till the sun rose over Magh Lifé on the morrow.

And through the length of seven years from that time, whenever he was not out fighting against the enemies of Ireland, he went searching and ever searching in every far corner for beautiful Sadbh. And there was great trouble on him all the time, unless he might throw it off for a while in hunting or in battle. And through all that time he never brought out to any hunting but the five hounds he had most trust in, Bran, and Sceolan and Lomaire and Brod and Lomluath, the way there would be no danger for Sadbh if ever he came on her track.

But after the end of seven years, Finn and some of his chief men were hunting on the sides of Beinn Gulbain, and they heard a great outcry among the hounds, that were gone into some narrow place. And when they followed them there, they saw the five hounds of Finn in a ring, and they keeping back the other hounds and in the middle of the ring was a young boy, with high looks, and he naked and having long hair. And he was no way daunted by the noise of the hounds, and did not look at them at all, but at the men that were coming up. And as soon as the fight was stopped Bran and Sceolan went up to the little lad, and whined and licked him, that any one would think they had forgotten their master. Finn and the others came up to him then, and put their hands on his head, and made much of him. And they brought him to their own hunting cabin, and he ate and drank with them, and before long he lost his wildness and was the same as themselves. And as to Bran and Sceolan, they were never tired playing about him.

And it is what Finn thought, there was some look of Sadbh in his face, and that it might be he was her son, and he kept him always beside

him. And little by little when the boy had
learned their talk, he told them all he could
remember. He used to be with a deer he loved
very much, he said, and that cared for and shel-
tered him, and it was in a wide place they used
to be, having hills and valleys and streams and
woods in it, but that was shut in with high cliffs
on every side, that there was no way of escape
from it. And he used to be eating fruits and
roots in the summer, and in the winter there
was food left for him in the shelter of a cave.
And a dark-looking man used to be coming to
the place, and sometimes he would speak to the
dear softly and gently, and sometimes with a
loud angry voice. But whatever way he spoke,
she would always draw away from him with the
appearance of great dread on her, and the man
would go away in great anger. And the last time
he saw the deer, his mother, the dark man was
speaking to her for a long time, from softness to
anger. And at the end he struck her with a hazel
rod, and with that she was forced to follow
him, and she looking back all the while at the
child, and crying after him that any one would
pity her. And he tried hard to follow after her,
and made every attempt, and cried out with
grief and rage, but he had no power to move,

74

and when he could hear his mother no more he fell on the grass and his wits went from him. And when he awoke it is on the side of the hill he was, where the hounds found him. And he searched a long time for the place where he was brought up, but he could not find it.

And the name the Fianna gave him was Oisin, and it is he was their maker of poems, and their good fighter afterwards.

6

The Best Men of the Fianna

And while Oisin was in his youth, Finn had
other good men along with him, and the best of
them were Goll, son of Morna, and Caoilte,
son of Ronan, and Lugaidh's Son.

As to Goll, that was of Connacht, he was
very tall and light-haired, and some say he was
the strongest of all the Fianna. Finn made a
poem in praise of him one time when some
stranger was asking what sort he was, saying
how hardy he was and brave in battle, and as
strong as a hound or as the waves, and with all
that so kind and so gentle, and open-handed
and sweet-voiced, and faithful to his friends.

And the chessboard he had was called Solus-
tairtech, the Shining Thing, and some of the
chessmen were made of gold, and some of them
silver, and each one of them was as big as the fist
of the biggest man of the Fianna; and after the
death of Goll it was buried in Slieve Baune.

And as to Caoilte, that was a grey thin man,

he was the best runner of them all. And he did a
good many great deeds; a big man of the Fomor
he killed one time, and he killed a five-headed
giant in a wheeling door, and another time he
made an end of an enchanted boar that no one
else could get near, and he killed a great stag
that had got away from the Fianna through
twenty-seven years. And another time he
brought Finn out of Teamhair, where he was
kept by force by the High King, because of
some rebellion the Fianna had stirred up. And
when Caoilte heard Finn had been brought
away to Teamhair, he went out to avenge him.
And the first he killed was Cuireach, a king of
Leinster that had a great name, and he brought
his head up to the hill that is above Buadhmaic.
And after that he made a great rout through Ireland, bringing sorrow into every house for the
sake of Finn, killing a man in every place, and
killing the calves with the cows.

And every door the red wind from the east
blew on, he would throw it open, and go in and
destroy all before him, setting fire to the fields,
and giving the wife of one man to another.

And when he came to Teamhair, he came to
the palace, and took the clothes off the door-
keeper, and he left his own sword that was

worn thin in the king's sheath, and took the king's sword that had great power in it. And he went into the palace then in the disguise of a servant, to see how he could best free Finn.

And when evening came Caoilte held the candle at the king's feast in the great hall, and after a while the king said: 'You will wonder at what I tell you, Finn, that the two eyes of Caoilte are in my candlestick.'

'Do not say that,' said Finn, 'and do not put

reproach on my people although I myself am your prisoner; for as to Caoilte,' he said, 'that is not the way with him, for it is a high mind he has, and he only does high deeds, and he would not stand serving with a candle for all the gold in the world.'

After that Caoilte was serving the King of Ireland with drink, and when he was standing beside him he gave out a high sorrowful lament. 'There is the smell of Caoilte's skin on that lament,' said the king. And when Caoilte saw he knew him he spoke out and he said: 'Tell me what way I can get freedom for my master.'

'There is no way to get freedom for him but by doing one thing,' said the king, 'and that is a thing you can never do. If you bring me together a couple of all the wild creatures of Ireland,' he said, 'I will give up your master to you then.'

When Caoilte heard him say that he made no delay, but he set out from Teamhair, and went through the whole of Ireland to do that work for the sake of Finn. It was with the flocks of birds he began, though they were scattered in every part, and from them he went on to the beasts. And he gathered together two of every sort, two ravens from Fiodh da Bheann; two wild ducks from Loch na Seillein; two foxes from Slieve Cuilinn; two wild oxen from Burren; two swans from blue Dobhran; two owls from the wood of Faradhruim; two polecats from the branchy wood on the side of Druim da Raoin, the Ridge of the Victories; two gulls from the strand of Loch Leith; four woodpeckers from white Brosna; two plovers from Carraigh Dhain; two thrushes from Leith Lomard; two wrens from Dun Aoibh; two herons from Corrain Cleibh; two eagles from Carraig of the stones; two hawks from Fiodh Chonnach; two sows from Loch Meilghe; two water-hens from Loch Erne; two moor-hens from Monadh Maith; two sparrow-hawks from Dubhloch; two stonechats from Magh Cuillean; two tomtits from Magh Tuallainn; two swallows from Sean Abhla; two cormorants from Ath Cliath; two wolves from Broit Cliathach; two blackbirds from the Strand of the Two Women; two roebucks from Luachair Ire; two pigeons from Ceas Chuir; two nightingales from Leiter Ruadh; two starlings from green-sided Teamhair; two rabbits from Sith Dubh Donn; two wild pigs from Cluaidh Chuir; two cuckoos from Drom Daibh; two lapwings from Leanain na Furraich; two woodcocks from Craobh Ruadh; two hawks from the Bright Mountain; two grey mice from Luimneach; two otters from the Boinn; two larks from the Great Bog; two bats from the Cave of the Nuts; two badgers from the province of Ulster; two landrail from the banks of the Sionnan; two wagtails from Port Lairrge; two curlews from the harbour of Gallimh; two hares from Muirthemne; two deer from Sith Buidhe; two peacocks from Magh Mell; two eels from Duth Dur; two goldfinches from Slieve na nEan; two birds of slaughter from Magh Bhuilg; two bright swallows from Granard; two redbreasts from the Great Wood; two rock-cod from Cala Chairge; two sea-pigs from the great sea; two wrens from Mios an Chuil; two salmon from Eas Mhuic Muirne; two clean deer from Gleann na Smoil; two cows from Magh Mor; two cats from the Cave of Cruachan; two sheep from Bright Sidhe Diobhlain; two pigs of the pigs of the son of Lir; a ram and a crimson sheep from Innis.

And along with all these he brought ten hounds of the hounds of the Fianna, and a horse and a mare of the beautiful horses of Manannan.

And when Caoilte had gathered all these, he brought them to the one place. But when he tried to keep them together, they scattered here and there from him; the raven went away southward, and that vexed him greatly, but he overtook it again in Gleann da Bheann, beside Loch Lurcan. And then his wild duck went away from him, and it was not easy to get it again, but he followed it through every stream to grey Accuill till he took it by the neck and brought it back, and it no way willing.

And indeed through the length of his life Caoilte remembered well all he went through that time with the birds, big and little, travelling over hills and ditches and striving to bring them with him, that he might set Finn his master free.

And when he came to Teamhair he had more to go through yet, for the king would not let him bring them in before morning, but gave him a house having nine doors in it to put them up for the night. And no sooner were they put in than they raised a loud screech all together, for a little ray of light was coming to them through fifty openings, and they were trying to make their escape. And if they were not easy in the house, Caoilte was not easy outside it, watching every door till the rising of the sun on the morrow.

And when he brought out his troop, the

name the people gave them was 'Caoilte's Rabble', and there was no wonder at all in that.

But all the profit the King of Ireland got from them was to see them together for that one time. For no sooner did Finn get his freedom than the whole of them scattered here and there, and no two of them went by the same road out of Teamhair.

And that was one of the best things Caoilte, son of Ronan, ever did. And another time he ran from the wave of Cliodna in the south to the wave of Rudraige in the north. And Colla his son was a very good runner too, and one time he ran a race backwards against the three battalions of the Fianna for a chessboard. And he won the race, but if he did, he went backward over Beinn Edair into the sea.

And very good hearing Caoilte had. One time he heard the King of the Luigne of Connacht at his hunting, and Blathmec that was with him said, 'What is that hunt, Caoilte?'

'A hunt of three packs of hounds,' he said, 'and three sorts of wild creatures before them. The first hunt,' he said, 'is after stags and large deer and the second hunt is after swift small hares, and the third is a furious hunt after heavy boars.'

'And what is the fourth hunt, Caoilte?' said Blathmec.

'It is the hunting of heavy-sided, low-bellied badgers.'

And then they heard coming after the hunt the shouts of the lads and of the readiest of the men and the serving-men that were best at carrying burdens. And Blathmec went out to see the hunting, and just as Caoilte had told him, that was the way it was.

And he understood the use of herbs, and one time he met with two women that were very downhearted because their husbands had gone from them to take other wives. And Caoilte gave them Druid herbs, and they put them in the water of a bath and washed in it, and the love of their husbands came back to them, and they sent away the new wives they had taken.

And as to Lugaidh's Son, that was of Finn's blood, and another of the best men of the Fianna, he was put into Finn's arms as a child, and he was reared up by Duban's daughter, that had reared eight hundred fighting men of the Fianna, till his twelfth year, and then she gave him all he wanted of arms and of armour, and he went to Chorraig Conluain and the mountains of Slieve Bladhma, where Finn and the Fianna were at that time.

And Finn gave him a very gentle welcome, and he struck his hand in Finn's hand, and made his agreement of service with him. And he stopped through the length of a year with the Fianna; but he was someway sluggish through all that time, so that under his leading not more than nine of the Fianna got to kill so much as a boar or a deer. And along with that, he used to beat both his servants and his hounds.

And at last the three battalions of the Fianna went to where Finn was, at the Point of the Fianna on the edge of Loch Lein, and they made their complaint against Lugaidh's Son, and it is what they said: 'Make your choice now, will you have us with you, or will you have Lugaidh's Son by himself.'

Then Lugaidh's Son came to Finn, and Finn asked him, 'What is it has put the whole of the Fianna against you?'

'By my word,' said the lad, 'I do not know the reason, unless it might be they do not like me to be doing my feats and casting my spears among them.'

Then Finn gave him an advice, and it is what he said: 'If you have a mind to be a good champ-

ion, be quiet in a great man's house; be surly in
the narrow pass. Do not beat your hound without cause; do not bring a charge against your
wife without having knowledge of her guilt; do
not hurt a fool in fighting, for he is without his
wits. Do not find fault with high-up persons;
do not stand up to take part in a quarrel; have
no dealings with a bad man or a foolish man.
Let two-thirds of your gentleness be shown to
women and to little children that are creeping
on the floor, and to men of learning that make
the poems, and do not be rough with the
common people. Do not give your reverence to
all; do not be ready to have one bed with your
companions. Do not threaten or speak big
words, for it is a shameful thing to speak stiffly
unless you can carry it out afterwards. Do not
forsake your lord so long as you live; do not
give up any man that puts himself under your
protection for all the treasures of the world. Do
not speak against others to their lord, that is not
work for a good man. Do not be a bearer of
lying stories, or a tale-bearer that is always
chattering. Do not be talking too much; do not
find fault hastily; however brave you may be,
do not raise factions against you. Do not be
going to drinking-houses, or finding fault with

old men; do not meddle with low people; this is right conduct I am telling you. Do not refuse to share your meat; do not have a niggard for your friend; do not force yourself on a great man or give him occasion to speak against you. Hold fast to your arms till the hard fight is well ended. Do not give up your opportunity, but with that follow after gentleness.'

That was good advice Finn gave, and he was well able to do that; for it was said of him that he had all the wisdom of a little child that is busy about the house, and the mother herself not understanding what he is doing; and that is the time she has most pride in him.

And as to Lugaidh's Son, that advice stayed always with him, and he changed his ways, and after a while he got a great name among the poets of Ireland and of Alban, and whenever they would praise Finn in their poems, they would praise him as well.

And Aoife, daugher of the King of Lochlann, that was married to Mal, son of Aiel, King of Alban, heard the great praise the poets were giving to Lugaidh's Son, and she set her love on him for the sake of those stories.

And one time Mal her husband and his young men went hunting to Slieve-mor-Monaidh in the north of Alban. And when he was gone Aoife made a plan in her sunny house where she was, to go over to Ireland, herself and her nine foster-sisters. And they set out and went over the manes of the sea till they came to Beinn Edair, and there they landed.

And it chanced on that day there was a hunting going on, from Slieve Bladhma to Beinn Edair. And Finn was in his hunting seat, and his fosterling, brown-haired Duibhruinn, beside him. And the little lad was looking about him on every side, and he saw a ship coming to the strand, and a queen with modest looks in the ship, and nine women along with her. They landed then, and they came up to where Finn was, bringing every sort of present with them, and Aoife sat down beside him. And Finn asked news of her, and she told him the whole story, and how she had given her love to Lugaidh's Son, and was come over the sea looking for him; and Finn made her welcome.

And when the hunting was over, the chief men of the Fianna came back to where Finn was, and every one asked who was the queen that was with him. And Finn told them her name, and what it was brought her to Ireland. 'We welcome her that made that journey,' said they all; 'for there is not in Ireland or in Alban a better man than the man she is come looking for, unless Finn himself.'

And as to Lugaidh's Son, it was on the far side of Slieve Bladhma he was hunting that day, and he was the last to come in. And he went into Finn's tent, and when he saw the woman beside him he questioned Finn the same as the others had done, and Finn told him the whole story. 'And it is to you she is come,' he said, 'and here she is to you out of my hand, and all the war and the battles she brings with her; but it will not fall heavier on you,' he said, 'than on the rest of the Fianna.'

And she was with Lugaidh's Son a month and a year without being asked for. But one day the three battalions of the Fianna were on the Hill of the Poet of Leinster, and they saw three armed battalions equal to themselves coming against them, and they asked who was bringing them.

'It is Mal, son of Aiel, is bringing them,' said Finn, 'to avenge his wife on the Fianna. And it is a good time they are come,' he said, 'when we are gathered together at the one spot.'

Then the two armies went towards one another, and Mal, son of Aiel, took hold of his arms, and three times he broke through the Fianna, and every time a hundred fell by him. And in the middle of the battle he and Lugaidh's Son met, and they fought against one another with spear and sword. And whether the fight was short or long, it was Mal fell by Lugaidh's Son at the last.

And Aoife stood on a hill near by, as long as the battle lasted. And from that out she belonged to Lugaidh's Son, and was a mother of children to him.

TALES OF IRISH ENCHANTMENT
Patricia Lynch

Patricia Lynch brings to this selection of classical Irish folktales for young people all the imagination and warmth for which she is renowned.

There are seven stories here: Midir and Etain, The Quest of the Sons of Turenn, The Swan Children, Deirdre and the Sons of Usna, Labra the Mariner, Cuchulain – The Champion of Ireland and The Voyage of Maeldun.

They lose none of their original appeal in the retelling and are as delightful today as when they were first told.

The stories are greatly enhanced by the immediacy and strength of Frances Boland's imaginative drawings.

ENCHANTED IRISH TALES
Patricia Lynch

Enchanted Irish Tales tells of ancient heroes and heroines, fantastic deeds of bravery, magical kingdoms, weird and wonderful animals... This new illustrated edition of classical folktales, retold by Patricia Lynch with all the imagination and warmth for which she is renowned, rekindles the age-old legends of Ireland, as exciting today as they were when first told. The collection includes:

- Conary Mór and the Three Red Riders
- The Long Life of Tuan Mac Carrell
- Finn Mac Cool and Fianna
- Oisin and The Land of Youth
- The Kingdom of The Dwarfs
- The Dragon Ring of Connla
- Mac Datho's Boar
- Ethne

IRISH FAIRY TALES
Michael Scott

'He found he was staring directly at a leprechaun. The small man was sitting on a little mound of earth beneath the shade of a weeping willow tree... The young man could feel his heart beginning to pound. He had seen leprechauns a few times before but only from a distance. They were very hard to catch, but if you managed at all to get hold of one...'

Michael Scott's exciting stories capture all the magic and mystery of Irish folklore. This collection of twelve fairy tales, beautifully and unusually illustrated, include:

The arrival of the Tuatha de Danann in Erin

The fairy horses	The King's secret
The crow goddess	The fairies' revenge
The wise woman's payment	The shoemaker and himself
The floating island	The sunken town

IRISH ANIMAL TALES
Michael Scott

'Have you ever noticed how cats and dogs sometimes sit up and look at something that is not there? Have you ever seen a dog barking at nothing? And have you ever wondered why? Perhaps it is because the animals can see the fairy folk coming and going all the time, while humans can only see the little People at certain times...'

This illustrated collection of Michael Scott's strange stories reveal a wealth of magical creatures that inhabit Ireland's enchanted animal kingdom. The tales tell of the king of the cats, the magical cows, the fox and the hedgehog, the dog and the leprechaun, March, April and the Brindled Cow, the cricket's tale... A collection to entrance readers, both young and old.

THE CHILDREN'S BOOK OF IRISH FAIRY TALES
PATRICIA DUNN

The five exciting stories in this book tell of the mythical, enchanted origins of Irish landmarks when the countryside was peopled with good fairies, wicked witches, gallant heroes and beautiful princesses.

Did you know that there are bright, shimmering lakes in Killarney concealing submerged castles, mountain peaks in Wexford created by magic, a dancing bush in Cork bearing lifesaving berries, the remains of a witch in a Kerry field and deer with silver and golden horns around Lough Gartan and Donegal?

These stories tell of extraordinary happenings long, long ago and show that evidence of these exciting events can still be seen today if you only take the time to look carefully.

STRANGE IRISH TALES FOR CHILDREN
Edmund Lenihan

Strange Irish Tales for Children is a collection of four hilarious stories, by seanchaí Edmund Lenihan, which will entertain and amuse children of all ages.

The stories tell of the adventures of the Fianna and about Fionn MacCumhail's journey to Norway in search of a blackbird. There is a fascinating tale about 'The Strange Case of Seán na Súl' whose job was to kidnap people to take them away to a magic island. 'Taoscán MacLiath and the Magic Bees' is a story about the exploits of this very famous druid and about how he packed his spell-books and took himself off to the conference held by the druids of the Seven Lands.

STORIES OF OLD IRELAND FOR CHILDREN
Edmund Lenihan

Long ago in Ireland there were men who used to travel to the four ends of the earth and few travelled farther than Fionn and the men of the Fianna during their many exciting adventures. In *Stories of Old Ireland for Children* we read about 'Fionn Mac Cumhail and Feathers of China', 'King Cormac's Fighting Academy', and 'Fionn and the Mermaids'.

THE FIRST BOOK OF IRISH MYTHS AND LEGENDS

Eoin Neeson

Eoin Neeson delves deep into the past and comes up with plenty of intrigue, romance and excitement in these stories about our Firbolg and Milesian forbears. He retells his stories with a directness and simplicity which make them refreshingly modern. *The First Book of Irish Myths and Legends* contains 'The Tale of the Children of Tuireann', 'The Wooing of Etain', 'The Combat at the Ford', and 'Deirdre and the Sons of Usna'.

THE SECOND BOOK OF IRISH MYTHS AND LEGENDS

Eoin Neeson

Again more fascinating legends from Eoin Neeson. Included are 'The Children of Lir', the classic story of 'Diarmuid and Grainne' and an unusual story about Cuchulainn.

THE CHILDREN'S BOOK OF IRISH FOLKTALES
Kevin Danaher

These tales are filled with the mystery and adventure of a land of lonely country roads and isolated farms, humble cottages and lordly castles, rolling fields and tractless bogs. The tell of giants and ghosts, of queer happenings and wondrous deeds, of fairies and witches and of fools and kings.

ULSTER FOLK STORIES
for Children
Paddy Tunney

'It was not Johnie's first time to go astray. He made the sign of the cross, took off his coat and put it on again inside out. Almost at once he saw a rock he recognised ... he went towards it. He could scarcely believe his eyes. there was a door in the rock and it was ajar!'

Paddy Tunney's exciting collection of stories is suitable for all ages – from 9 to 90 – who enjoy a good story. In it we meet a whole host of interesting people.

IRISH FAIRY STORIES
for Children
Edmund Leamy

In these stories we read all about the exciting adventures of Irish children in fairyland. We meet the fairy minstrel, giants, leprechauns, fairy queens and wonderful talking animals in Tir na nÓg.